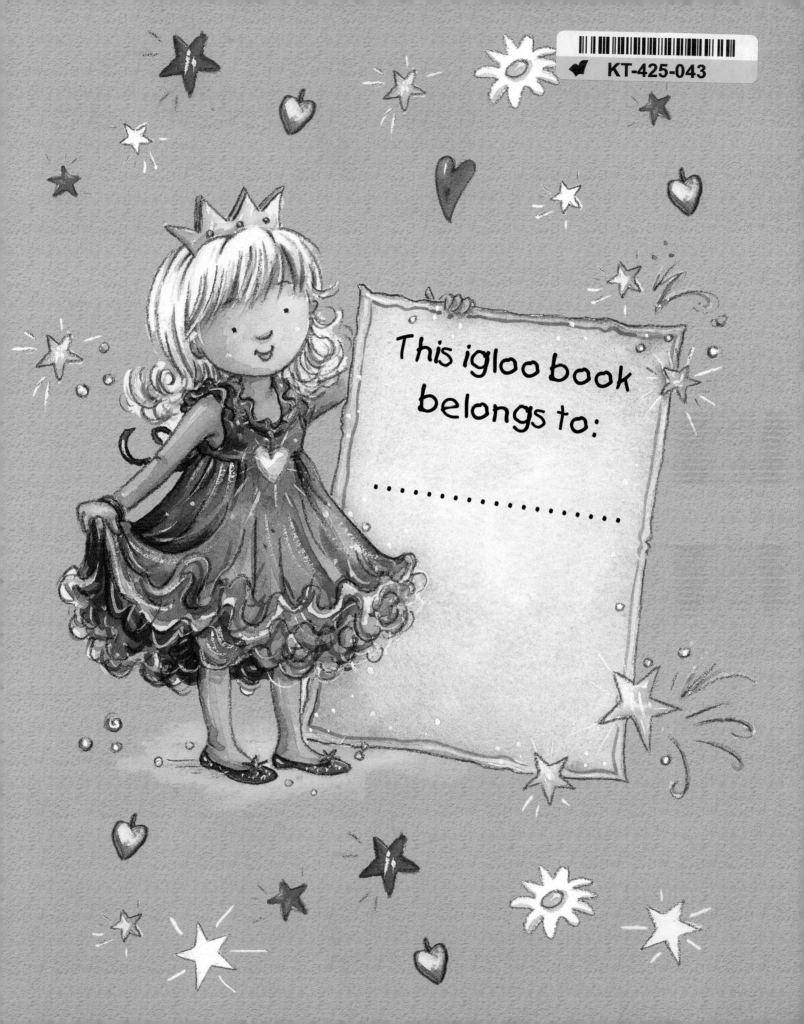

This igloo book belongs to:

.............................

Published in 2019
by Igloo Books Ltd
Cottage Farm
Sywell
NN6 OBJ
www.igloobooks.com

0719 001.01
4 6 8 10 9 7 5 3
ISBN: 978-0-85780-433-4

Project Managed by Insight Design Concepts Ltd.
Printed and manufactured in China

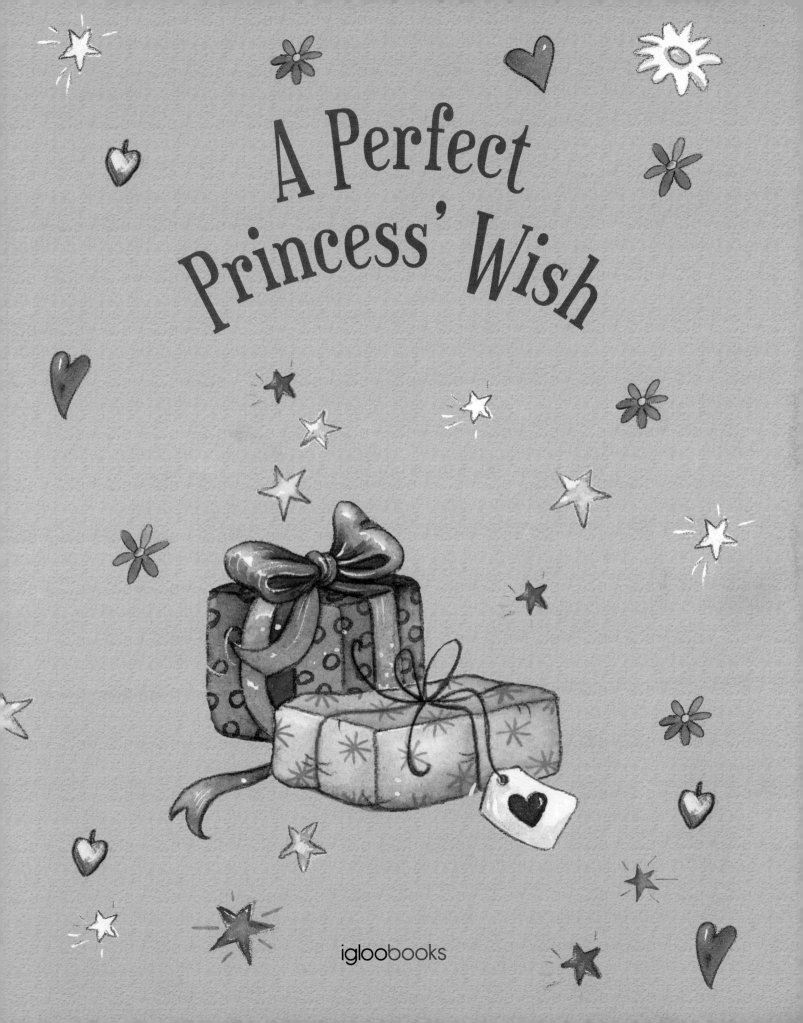

# A Perfect Princess' Wish

igloobooks

It was Princess Sophie's birthday and her godmother had sent her a special present.

'To Sophie,' said the label on the package. Open this box and look inside. There's a special locket where you can hide secret wishes, written by you. Then wait and they'll magically come true.'

Princess Sophie opened the box. Inside, just as the note said, there was a beautiful, heart-shaped locket.

Wondering if the locket really could make wishes come true, Princess Sophie found some paper and a pencil. In small, neat letters, she wrote: 'I wish I could have cupcakes for breakfast.' She folded her note and slipped it inside the locket. Then, she put on the locket and ran downstairs, ignoring the rest of the presents piled up in her bedroom.

"Happy Birthday, Your Highness," said the palace butler, when Princess Sophie sat down at the breakfast table. She held her breath as he carried out the silver tray that usually held sausages, or porridge. "Raspberry cupcakes, Your Highness," said the butler, placing the tray in front of her, "with chocolate sprinkles." Princess Sophie was so surprised, she almost fell off her throne.

As soon as she had finished breakfast, Princess Sophie went back to her bedroom. She had some serious thinking to do about her next wish.

Everyone in the palace was busy preparing for her birthday party and, as she heard them bustling about, it gave her an idea.

She wrote her wish on a scrap of paper, then put it inside the locket. It said, 'I wish for fireworks at my birthday party.'

The royal birthday party was a terrific success. Princess Sophie and her friends danced, played games and drank pink lemonade.
As everyone sang "Happy Birthday", there was a sudden bang! outside the palace windows. The sky was filled with fireworks.
Princess Sophie giggled, because her second wish had come true.

That night, Princess Sophie found it hard to fall asleep. She sat up in bed, staring at the magic locket on her dressing table. Could it hurt to make one more wish? She crept across the room in her bare feet. 'I wish it could be my birthday every day,' she wrote on a piece of paper. She slipped the wish inside the locket.

The next morning, Princess Sophie woke up and looked at the end of her bed. There was a huge pile of shiny, wrapped gifts, just as there had been the day before. Princess Sophie was amazed. "Presents!" she cried, excitedly.

The following day, after she'd opened her newest pile of birthday presents, Princess Sophie went to find the king. "May I go for a pony ride?" she asked.
"Absolutely not," replied the king. "Your party guests will be here soon. You must be ready when they arrive."
Princess Sophie frowned. She wanted to be outdoors with her pony, not stuck inside playing party games.

At breakfast the next morning, Princess Sophie asked the butler, "Can I have toast this morning?"
"These cupcakes are a special birthday treat, Your Highness," said the butler, putting down the silver tray. Princess Sophie scowled. She wanted toast and marmalade, not cupcakes again.

After a whole week of birthdays, Princess Sophie was royally miserable. With birthday celebrations every day, she couldn't ride her pony, or go to ballet lessons, or do any of the things she normally enjoyed. Her bedroom was so full of presents, there wasn't even room to play anymore.

She was very worried too. If every day was her birthday, did that mean all other holidays were cancelled? What about the fabulous summer ball that was held at the palace every year?

Princess Sophie felt as though she had nothing to look forward to,
except more cupcakes and party games. "I wish everything would
go back to normal," thought Princess Sophie.
And then she remembered the locket.
She hunted through the enormous pile of presents in her bedroom
until she finally found the heart-shaped locket.

'I wish for just one birthday a year,' she wrote in her neatest handwriting.

She folded up the note and put it inside the locket. Then, she tucked the locket under her pillow and fell asleep.

I wish for just one birthday a year

When she woke up the next morning, there were no new presents in her bedroom.

Princess Sophie smiled. "My wish has come true!" she cried.

"Toast and marmalade, Your Highness," said the butler, putting the silver tray down when she arrived at the breakfast table.

Princess Sophie was very happy.

It was a whole year until her next birthday, thought Princess Sophie, as she headed out for a pony ride, but she didn't mind one little bit.